Baldwinsville Public Library
East Genesee Street
P9-DGW-777

P9-DGW-777

FOR
snodgrass
aND THE
FiSH
(those TWO
FAMOUS
GRiNNeRs)

MAR 0 9 2010

Balzer & Bray is an imprint of HarperCollins Publishers.

Smile!
Copyright © 2009 by Leigh Hodgkinson
All rights reserved. Manufactured in China.
No part of this book may be used or reproduced in any manner whatsoever without written permission except in the case of brief quotations embodied in critical articles and reviews.

For information address HarperCollins Children's Books, a division of HarperCollins Publishers, 10 East 53rd Street, New York, NY 10022. www.harpercollinschildrens.com

Library of Congress Cataloging-in-Publication Data is available.
ISBN 978-0-06-185269-5

10 11 12 13 14 HLUK 10 9 8 7 6 5 4 3 2 1

First U.S. edition, 2010
Originally published in Great Britain by Orchard Books in 2009

Baldwinsville Public Library
WITHDRAWN

smile!

Leigh Hodgkinson

BALZER + BRAY
An Imprint of HarperCollins Publishers

Mom says I can't have ANY MORE cookies until dinner. (And that includes CRUMBS and little broken pieces.)

By the way, I am DEFINITELY NOT sulking.

I am NOT particularly chipper or chirpy either. Usually THESE things are ME in a nutshell, but not today. This is because I've just realized something

TERRIBLE!

I have LOST something V e R y,
VERY IMPO R tANT.
What I've LOST is my SMILE.
I wish I could find it.

If I had my smile, everything would
be very nice and normal indeed.

See, I **L♥V℮** to smile!
Smiling is one of my favorite hobbies.
Smiling makes me feel SUNSHINY
and as fresh as a daisy,
WHATEVER the weather!

SPLOSH

My dad says I should try to REMEMBER where I last saw it.

And I think,
RIDICULOUS!

If I knew THAT, then it wouldn't be LOST, would it?

Dad says I will just have to look for it.

BUT looking for things is <u>SO</u> <u>BORING.</u>
IF I was a **MULTI-EYED ALIEN**,
finding lost things would be SUPER speedy.
I'm not a **MULTI-EYED ALIEN**, though.

I'm just me.

Maybe my smile has fallen under my bed. So I LOOK, but it ISN'T there!
(Even though

EVERYTHING

else seems to be.)

Perhaps I dropped it on the FLOOR?
If there IS a floor under all this stuff!
I don't think I have ever seen it.
It COULD be an ocean made of
WIBBLY WOBBLY Jell-O
for all I know.

RASPBERRY
JELLYFISH

I suppose I had better CLEAN UP.
This is HIGHLY UNUSUAL,
but I'm

DESPERATE!

doggy PADDLE

No smile to report here.
Only one UN-higgledy-piggledy
bedroom and NO Jell-O.

But what if I didn't LOSE my smile?
What if SOMEBODY took it?

Well, I don't think it was Glittergills.

Cheer up,
Glittergills!

Maybe a sprinkle of fishy flakes will do the trick?

AHA!

Maybe the TWINS took it?
They ask me what I'm up to,
so I tell them — and they just

giggle.

However, I don't think they're to blame (this time) as their smiles are much BIGGER than mine and MUCH more ANNOYING.

MY smile is EXACTLY the right shape and size for

just me!

It simply wouldn't suit

ANYBODY else.

So, if it ISN'T in my bedroom and it HASN'T been stolen . . .

it must be LOST in the
BIG WIDE WORLD.

But it will take **AGES**
to look there. . . .

Maybe I'll quickly check
the rest of our house first.

Mom says that **MOST** lost things in this house can be found in the following places:

1. The sofa

2. Pocket

Exhibit

3. MR. HONEYCOMB'S bASket

Oh, look!
One of Dad's
FLIP-FLOPs.

(I think this is
the FLOP one.)

tHe DOGHOUSE

Well, seeing as I am here, I'll just have a quick game with Mr. Honeycomb.

FIVE games later,
Mom finds me and says that
my SPIC -and- SPAN
room is a COMPLETE

miracle!
She ALSO says that I am
a SWEET PEA for feeding
Glittergills and playing with
Mr. Honeycomb.

I think 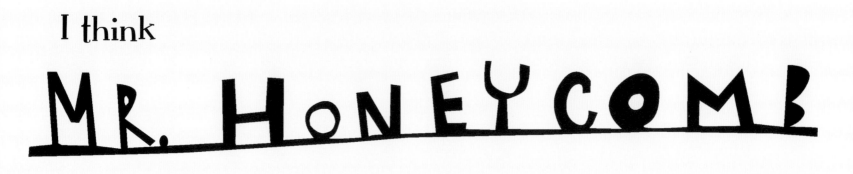 agrees!

"You've found it!"
say the twins.

And I say, "**FOUND WHAT?**"

"We **KNEW** it would turn up!" say the twins.

And I say,
"<u>Knew</u> <u>**WHAT**</u> WOULD TURN **UP?**"

and THEY say . . .

Smiling.